MW01123324

For my grandmother, whose heart continues to nurture, comfort, and inspire me in immeasurable ways.

www.mascotbooks.com

Benvolio's Heart

For more information, please contact:
Mascot Books
620 Herndon Parkway, Suite 320
Herndon, VA 20170
info@mascotbooks.com

Library of Congress Control Number: 2018902817

CPSIA Code: PRT0518A
ISBN-13: 978-1-68401-905-2

Printed in the United States

Benvolio's Heart

When Pure Love Spills From the Inside Out

ANTHONY
ZOMPARELLI

Illustrated by
TOBY MIKLE

From the very second that Benvolio burst out into the world, his heart was singing. It was thumping and glowing and singing a song of love that everyone around him could hear loud and clear.

Benvolio's mother picked up her baby boy, placed her hand on his chest, and looked into his bright eyes. "You have an extraordinary heart, baby boy. It will help change the world in beautiful ways."

As a little boy, Benvolio had a special way of giving his heart to people. He used his heart to fix things for the people he cared about. First, his heart would guide him to the person who was hurt or in trouble. Then, he'd cheer them up until they smiled wide. Benvolio would spread love and goodness to everyone he came across.

For Benvolio, sharing the love in his heart was as easy as breathing is for most people.

Instead of playing outside or watching TV, Benvolio sang sweet songs to his baby sister so she would stop crying and fall asleep. He was always happy to help his mom.

Or if his friends had nothing left to eat, Benvolio shared the last bit of his snack. He didn't mind being hungry. It felt good to feed his friends.

Some years, he would even blow out his own birthday cake candles and make a wish for someone else. He felt that he had everything he needed, so he thought, *Why shouldn't someone else out there have the same?*

While many of the boys and girls around him played basketball, practiced piano, or focused on other activities, Benvolio knew what was most important to him: exercising his heart by letting it give and do as much good as possible.

Benvolio's father would often say to him, "My son, your heart marches ten steps ahead of you. You will never be able to catch it!"

"Should I get my heart a pair of running shoes then?" Benvolio would always joke. But the truth was that Benvolio never quite understood what his dad meant.

One day, he finally asked his parents, "If a person's heart is on the inside, how can it be ten steps ahead on the outside?"

Benvolio's parents chuckled. "It's just a way of saying something," his dad said. "We call it an *expression*. Your heart doesn't actually leave your body. That'd be impossible!"

"But then what does it mean?" Benvolio asked, eyes wide.

"The love in your heart can travel as far as it needs to," his dad continued. "So, it's the goodness in that heart of yours that can spread to people and places far from where you are."

Benvolio tried to understand. "Is that what happened when I closed my eyes tight and sent Nanna great big hugs and kisses all the way to London so she would feel better?"

"That is exactly what happened, Benvolio," said his mom. "Your heart holds many messages, and you can deliver them in *words*, *actions*, and even *thoughts*. The love in your heart can reach anyone and any place."

Benvolio thought about this for a little while. "So, have I been using my heart in the right way?"

"Of course you have, but there are always new lessons to learn," explained his dad. "It's very easy for you to give your heart to the people you love, but sometimes, a heart like yours has to be shared with people who have not been so nice to you."

Benvolio was confused. "Do you mean the people who are my..." Benvolio did not even want to say the word. He did not like the word and he especially didn't like the sound of it. Finally, he whispered, "...enemies?"

"No, that's not what I mean," his mom said. "I'm talking about the people who haven't learned how important love is. Do you know any of those people, Benvolio?"

Benvolio wanted to look away. His heart could tell that his mother knew about the problems he was having at school.

"I spoke with your teacher today. She told me about a boy named Liam in your class."

Benvolio's eyes began to shed tears. It hurt to think about what was happening at school. It hurt in his head, his stomach, and mostly, in his heart.

For weeks, Liam had been bullying Benvolio. He would take Benvolio's food at lunchtime and eat it right in front of him. He even stole marbles out of Benvolio's desk and pretended he knew nothing about it. Benvolio couldn't understand why anyone would treat him, or anyone, that way.

His mother held him close. "It's all going to get fixed. The solution is in your heart."

Benvolio sat up in his bed that night, leaning against his fluffy pillows. The only person he could think about was Liam. It made him more *sad* than *mad* to think about Liam. Benvolio knew in his mighty heart that Liam needed something from him. And that something was love. Benvolio wondered how he could use his heart and the *love* inside of it to wake up *Liam's* heart. There had to be a way.

Benvolio closed his eyes and remembered what his father said about his heart marching fast ahead of him. *That was it!* He would send his heart to Liam, and he'd do it right now. He concentrated hard, and off it went. Benvolio's heart was on a mission. But even as it went, he knew there was still work to be done.

Benvolio listened closely to the whisper of his heart and he knew exactly what he would have to do tomorrow at school. It wasn't going to be easy, but he knew he could do it.

It was lunchtime at school, and Benvolio had never felt so nervous about eating lunch. Usually Liam would take his lunch away from him at this exact time. But today, Benvolio still had his lunch with him. Liam hadn't taken it. Something was already working.

Guided by that special heart of his, Benvolio found Liam in the cafeteria sitting alone and not eating a single thing. Benvolio reached inside his backpack and pulled out a brown paper bag with a name on it. It read, **L-I-A-M**. Inside the bag, Benvolio had packed all of the food and treats that Liam had been stealing from him. Benvolio knew they were his favorites. He placed the bag before Liam and then reached for his own lunch.

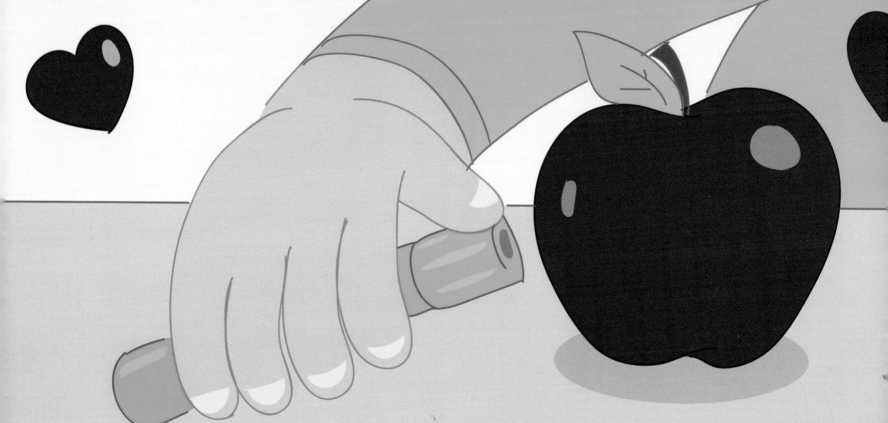

Benvolio did this the next day and the day after that. Every time, he found Liam in the lunchroom, sat across from him with a smile, and presented him with a brown paper bag lunch. All of the other children, and even some of the teachers, looked on with confusion. Everyone wondered why Benvolio was doing what he was doing, but Benvolio didn't explain it to anyone. The two boys ate together without saying a word.

But one day, before Benvolio could even put the brown paper bag down, Liam stood up with his hand raised in a fist. He looked straight into Benvolio's eyes.

Benvolio felt shaky and a little bit sweaty. He was trying hard to trust his heart, but he couldn't help but wonder if his heart had put him in a scary situation.

Liam slowly released his hand from a fist to an open palm. But Liam's palm was not empty. It was full of the marbles he had taken from Benvolio!

"These belong to you," Liam said. "I should never have taken them. I'm sorry."

Benvolio counted the marbles and noticed that there were ones he had never seen before.

"Thanks Liam," said Benvolio. "But not all of these belong to me."

"They do now," said Liam. "These are three of my favorite marbles and I want you to have them."

Benvolio was puzzled. "But why?" he asked.

"You're the only kid in this whole school who sat down to eat with me...even after I was mean to you. I thought you were looking for a fight, but you brought me lunch instead," explained Liam. "I didn't know how much I was missing by not having a friend until you helped me. It feels way better to be kind than it does to be mean.
If it were up to me, you'd be getting three marbles every day this school year."

Both boys laughed but Liam did something he'd hadn't done in a long time. He cried. As he reached his hand out to his new friend, Liam let the tears trapped in him for so long trickle down his cheeks. He was finally feeling the true joy of friendship and what it felt like to share his own heart.

"I didn't think I'd ever find a friend at this school," said Liam. "No one has ever been nice to me the way you have."

Benvolio smiled. He was glad that he had trusted his heart. Giving his heart to Liam was the only way that Liam could discover his very own heart.

"You found more than just a friend, Liam...you've found your heart."

Benvolio's heart says:

"You should always use your heart to help unlock someone else's heart."

ABOUT THE AUTHOR

Benvolio's Heart is Anthony Zomparelli's second children's book. He is also the author of *No Fangs Fillmore*. Anthony works in the area of education and uses literacy instruction to work toward his goal of making even the youngest readers aware of their social responsibilities and impact. Anthony sincerely hopes that *Benvolio's Heart* will inspire all readers to become ambassadors of kindness while using their hearts to help the planet become an even better place.

Have a book idea?
Contact us at:

info@mascotbooks.com | www.mascotbooks.com